Global Warming? Global Warning!
Copyright © 2024 by Jeanne C Rosenbohm

Published in the United States of America

Library of Congress Control Number: 2024925953
ISBN   Paperback: 979-8-89091-771-3
ISBN   eBook: 979-8-89091-772-0

All rights reserved. No part of this publication may be reproduced, stored in a retrieval system or transmitted in any way by any means, electronic, mechanical, photocopy, recording or otherwise without the prior permission of the author except as provided by USA copyright law.

The opinions expressed by the author are not necessarily those of ReadersMagnet, LLC.

ReadersMagnet, LLC
10620 Treena Street, Suite 230 | San Diego, California, 92131 USA
1.619. 354. 2643 | www.readersmagnet.com

Book design copyright © 2024 by ReadersMagnet, LLC. All rights reserved.

Cover design by Ericka Obando
Interior design by Don De Guzman

GLOBAL WARMING?

GLOBAL WARNING!

JEANNE C ROSENBOHM

AUTHOR'S NOTE FOR GLOBAL WARMING

The First Earth Day was celebrated in 1970. I was a first year teacher still too timid to peek beyond our teacher's editions that provided us with all the questions and answers we would ever need to ask.

It took a couple of years to get my teacher boots on to find material to complement the lessons. That is when I first taught Earth Day.

I arranged for the viewing of a program on pollution and recycling that had been shown on our local PBS channel. They agreed to rebroadcast it during the day at a time designated for our science class. This was a big deal back then.

Since then, I've wanted to express how I feel about Mother Earth and to wake up those people who still have no interest or no desire to do anything about this topic. The time has come for us to decide if we want to help …or not.

Earth Day has celebrated over 50 years of being able to celebrate Mother Earth. Please help the earth thrive 100 years from now.

Make a choice.

GLOBAL WARMING?

GLOBAL WARNING!

GLOBAL WARNING!

GLOBAL WARMING?

FROM WHAT I'M LEARNING ABOUT WHAT THEY SAY

THE WORLD TEMPERATURE'S CLIMBING DAY BY DAY

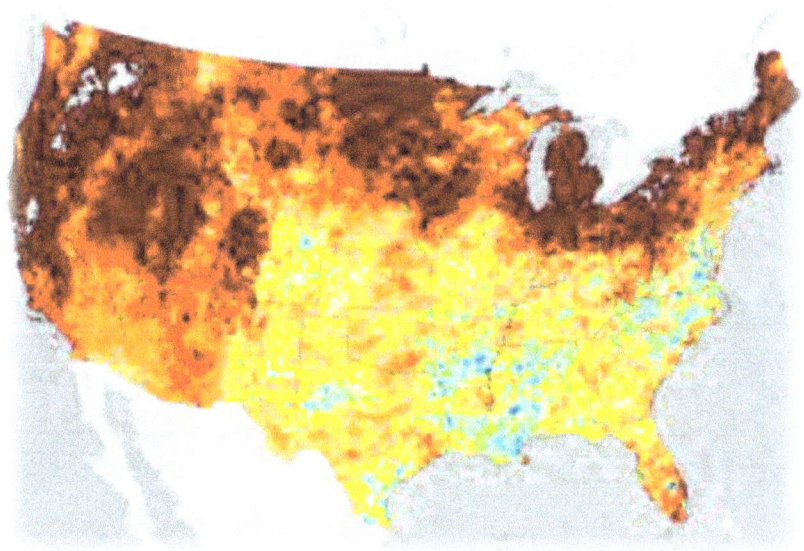

THE WATER AT SEA LEVEL IS A RISIN'

COULD LUBBOCK BEACH SUNSETS BE ON THE HORIZON?

WHAT'S THAT? YOU'RE HUNGRY?

YOU WANT A LITTLE BEEF?

DRIVE UP TO THE FIELD OUT BY THE DEAD REEF

YOU'LL SEE A HERD OF HOT COWS STANDING IN CLUMPS

YOU CAN CARVE YOUR BURGERS RIGHT OFF OF THEIR RUMPS

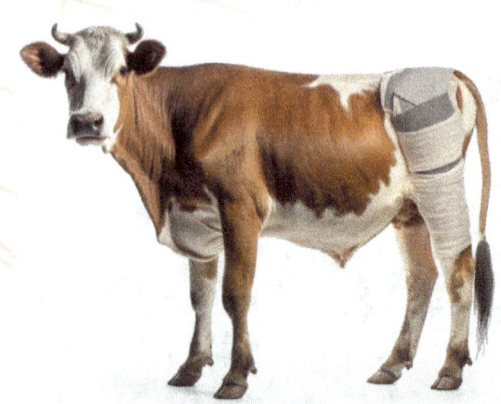

GLOBAL WARNING!
GLOBAL WARMING?

GLOBAL WARMING? GLOBAL WARNING!

YOU'RE THIRSTY? YOU WANT TO DRINK SOMETHING COLD?

WELL, WE CAN SERVE YOU, IF YOU'LL BE A LITTLE BOLD WHEN YOU SEE THE ICEBERG COME FLOATING BY

GRAB A BUCKET OF ICE CHIPS ON THE FLY

DISEASE CARRYING MOSQUITOES ARE ON THEIR WAY

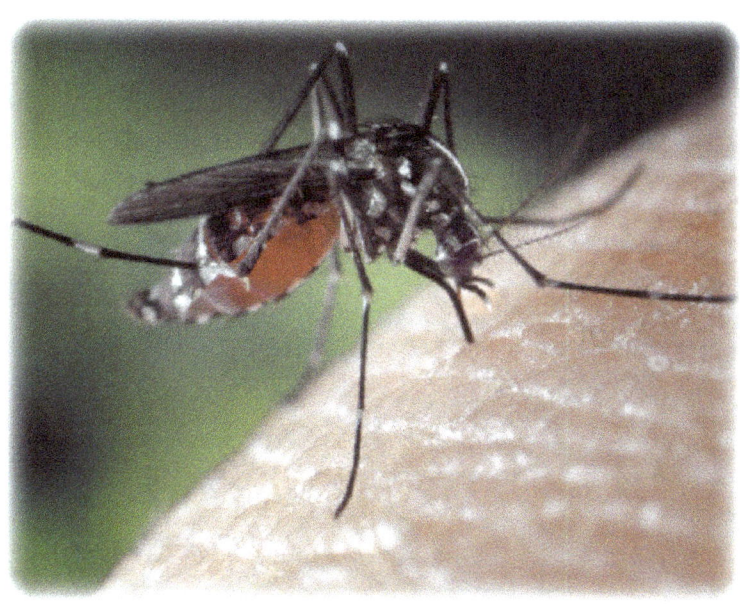

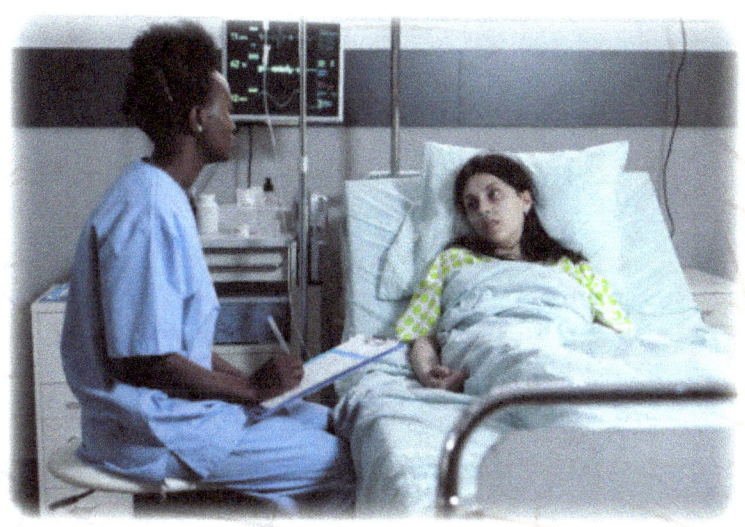

WHEN DENGUE FEVER'S COMMON THERE'LL BE DUES TO PAY.

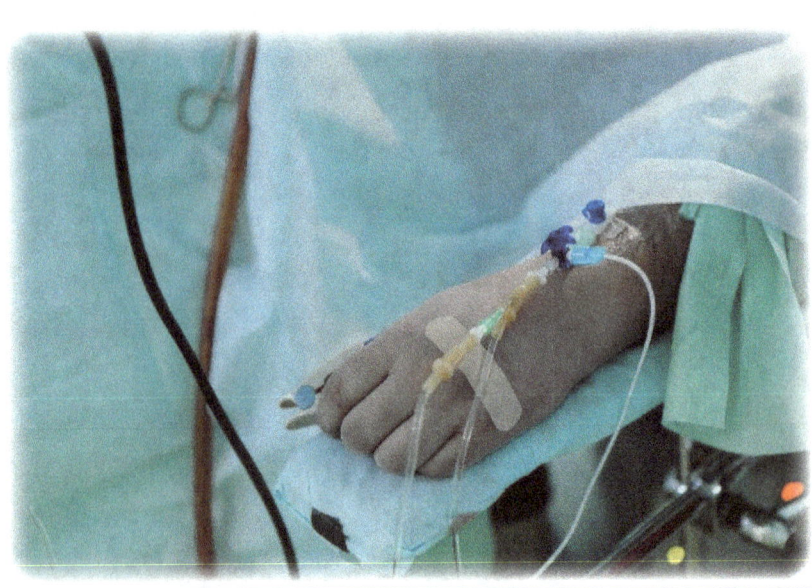

HOW DENGUE COULD SPREAD IN A WARMING WORLD

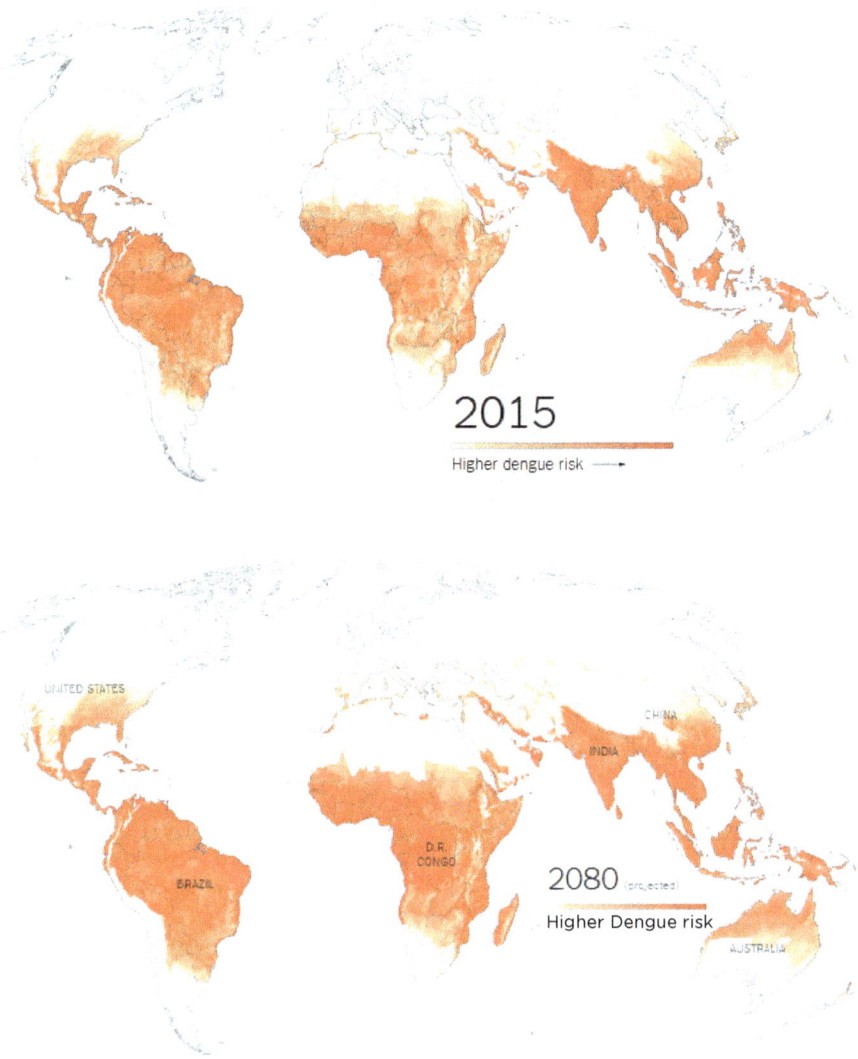

The 2080 map data is modeled using a climate scenario under which the world is likely to exceed 2 degrees Celsius warning by the end of the century compared with the pre-industrial times.
Source: Messina, Brady et al. Nature Microbiology

IF YOU WALK OUTSIDE AND GET MALARIA

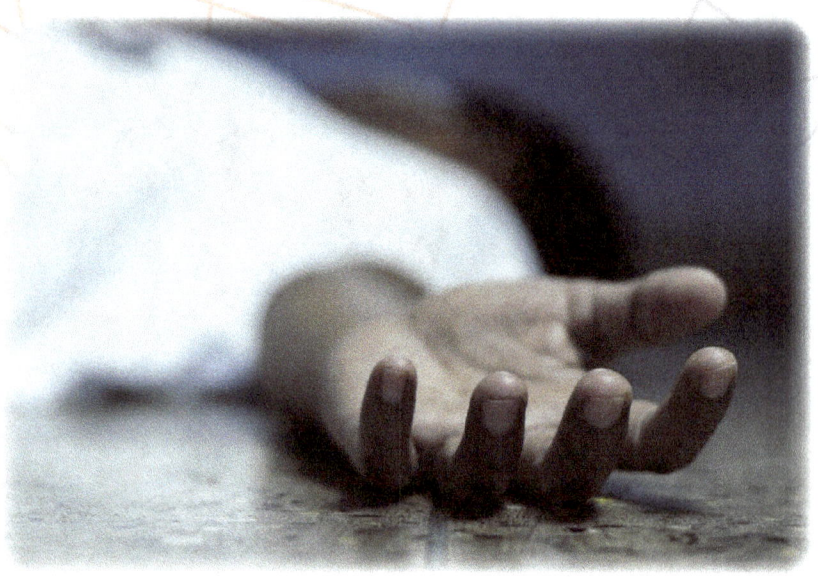

PLEASE MAKE SURE SOMEONE'S LEFT TO BURY YA'

HURRICANES INCREASING IN NUMBER

BEETLES IN ALASKA CHEWING UP THE LUMBER

SEVERE DROUGHTS IN THE SOUTH AND WEST

FLOODS IN THE EAST

27

COULD WE BE APPROACHING THE BELLY OF THE BEAST?

GLOBAL WARMING?

29

GLOBAL WARNING!

CLIMATE CHANGE!

WHAT DO YOU THINK?

MAKE A CHOICE!

What do you believe about global warming?

Are you doing anything personally to help the earth?

Do you know what the air pollution organizations have done to clean the air you breathe and how much CO2 is in the air?

How much do you know about CO2 emissions in your area? Do you live near a manufacturing company or a major highway?

What do the people in your community think about electric cars to cut back on gasoline consumption? (Consumption means using it)

What do the people believe about not producing as much oil and coal for use in power plants?

Are trees being clear cut around you to provide land for businesses?

How are trees related to global warming?

Do you know anyone who uses solar panels for energy? What do you think about them?

Some people believe human beings should take the responsibility of being stewards of the earth. What is a steward? In what ways can you be a steward?

Many indigenous people (those who have always lived on the land where they are) believe human beings are responsible for the lives of the next seven generations. What do you believe?

What do you know about Earth Day? Can you think of ways you could get involved?

What else do we have to start doing to save the earth in addition to acting to slow global warming? How about stopping water pollution? How about helping people organize recycling days? Shredding days? Anti-litter days?

What does being in the belly of the beast mean?

There is much you can do. Mother Earth depends on you.

Cultures believe they have a right to use the land however they choose and never think of the impact of their actions. Some cultures believe they have obligations to preserve the earth for future generations.

What you believe could initiate the healing or lead the world into destruction.

www.ingramcontent.com/pod-product-compliance
Lightning Source LLC
LaVergne TN
LVHW020416070526
838199LV00054B/3636